The Fall of Jacintha

F. A. Witte

Published by F.A. Witte, 2023.

This is a work of fiction. Similarities to real people, places, or events are entirely coincidental.

THE FALL OF JACINTHA

First edition. November 17, 2023.

Copyright © 2023 F. A. Witte.

ISBN: 979-8215389782

Written by F. A. Witte.

To my sister Krystal. You have always been a big support in whatever I chose to do in life. Incuding this dream. I could never repay you for your graditude, kindness, love and support. I love you sister.

Chapter One

When I was three and my sister Aleeta barely two, there was a great battle in our Kingdom. I don't remember much of it. I remember being locked in the dungeon with my mother, sister, and other children and women from the kingdom. When we were finally allowed to come out, there were still things on fire. It was almost impossible to breathe with all the smoke. I can remember being grabbed by one of the knights. He held me tight in one arm and my sister in another. I kicked and screamed for him to let me go. I didn't know where he was taking us, and I couldn't see anything past the smoke. I could hear women screaming and children crying. Or vice versa. I was scared and I wanted my father, King Kornel. The more I screamed the more smoke got into my lungs and it was starting to get harder to breathe. Right before I passed out the knight let me go and I woke up in my father's arms.

We had to relocate after our home was burnt to ash. I remember traveling for weeks until my father found the safest spot for us all. I remember being starving and dirty. I hated being away from home. At least the place that used to be home.

"This is it!" my father exclaimed. "This is where we will rebuild."

There was chatter from all around. The people were pleased. Looking at the area, there were all trees. Just a bunch of trees.

"We rest tonight and tomorrow we start to build the best kingdom there ever was."

Several of the village survivors followed their king to new grounds. That night we feasted on what animals were hunted nearby. A big fire was placed in the center of us all. Everyone laughed and danced around the fire. I remember it being one of the best nights.

That next day my father and the survivors did as they said they would. They started to build. One by one the trees came down. Men worked from sunup to sundown. It gave Aleeta and I a chance to run around with the other kids. The women helped out when us kids weren't being too much of a handful.

It took several years to build from the ground up. Those who helped my father with labor got to stay in the castle with their families and live like royalty as their reward for being loyal. Their wives and daughter's learned to sew, and their sons would learn to be knights.

Dateron is what my father named our new kingdom. It was the most beautiful place I had ever seen after it was built. It was secluded by tall tree's still, which made it hard for anyone to find us in the beginning. The population started out small due to all the men we lost in battle but has grown over time. Hidden in the mountains surrounded by trees and rivers. There was a waterfall behind the castle where my sister, Aletta and I liked to play when we were younger. My favorite place to go to get lost in my dreams when I got older. During the spring, the surroundings really came alive. The trees fully bloomed and the land a beautiful bright green. Flowers of yellow, pink, purple, and blue blossomed all around us. It felt magical being there in the beginning. Eventually, that would all change.

Just outside the castle, beyond the tree's, was a village, Rosewich. I dreamed of one day going there and exploring what was beyond the kingdom's walls but, our father has forbidden us to ever leave the castle. We were prisoners in our own home. For good reason if you ask him.

At the age of eleven my mother, Queen Tianna, was killed by one of the survivors my father welcomed to stay with us. It was a dark time for me and my sister. My father seeked his revenge and the reasoning for her murder. I saw my mother minutes before she was killed, and I pointed the guy out to my father. He was beheaded for his crimes in front of everyone. He claimed his innocence until his last breath. We never did know why our mother's life was taken.

Our father became overprotective of us. He was scared someone would try to hurt me or my sister. He banned everyone from the kingdom except the sons that were training to be knights. That's when Rosewich was built. By the people my father turned his back on because of the death if his queen. Sometimes when I like out my window, I can see a glimpse of the fire at night. They were probably dancing and laughing like we used to do. We never got to do that anymore.

Our father made us train with the knights under the command of Hendriick. Not to prepare us for battle, but to protect ourselves from harm. He wanted us to know how to defend ourselves if someone ever tried to hurt us. At first, I hated it. I felt like we were being punished for our mother's death. Over the years I became so good that I would help Hendriick with the training. I was one of the best with a sword. I'd rather be training than making dresses. I guess I had my reasons now.

Aletta, on the other hand, had no interest for it. She wasn't focused enough, and she'd get caught off guard every time. It was the one thing I could do better than my sister. She was your typical girly princess. Wore the prettiest, bright colored dresses. She had her own tailor from the village that handmade dresses just for her. Our father spoiled her rotten. She was so beautiful it made me sick how everyone would just drool over her. Her long curly blonde hair was perfect every day and her sparkling blue eyes hypnotized every man she met. She was the perfect likeness to our mother, and our father kept her close.

As for me, I was my father's daughter. Brown eyes and hair. I had a scar alongside my face from my ear to my chin. It happened when we were younger. Aletta and I were playing by the waterfall when she pushed me in. Why she pushed me, I don't know. I heard her laugh as I screamed on the way down. I fell ten feet and my face was stricken by a sharp rock at the bottom. I didn't know how to swim and if it wasn't for Hendriick I wouldn't be alive today. So now I live in the shadows of my sister who did this to me. Being in armor and training with the knights made me feel as if I were one of them. They all had battle wounds, and I didn't feel so insecure with them.

Chapter Two

I sat in my room at the edge of the window looking out. The sun was setting behind the mountain my room was facing. I could hear armor clacking together in the distance. Must be the knights finishing their training for the day. I had missed training the past couple of days. Too busy in my own dream world. Trying to figure out a way to escape my own hell. My room was high enough to barely see over the castle wall. I could see far into the distance. Just right before the mountain. Farms were lined up neatly in a row. Occasionally, I could see the farmers collecting their crops. One day I hoped to see more than just farms. I often wondered what their lives were like. Were they prisoners in their own home as well? Or their lives were more of a fairy tale than mine were. Some nights you can hear music coming from the village and laughter from the village people. They sounded happy and free. I wanted to laugh like them and be free like them. I imagined the women in fancy dresses and the men dressed in their Sunday best dancing the night away. Oh, what I would give to spend one night like that. A night away from the castle. Away from my sister and father. Away from this prison where everyone looked at me like I was some disgusting creature.

My distraction broke when I heard a creak. I knew someone was approaching me slowly. My sword was laid out beside me, and I gripped the handle with both hands and swung it as I turned around. It stopped in midair when it clashed with another sword.

"Princess, you are getting better." It was Hendriick. He was still in some of his armor and his long black hair was pulled back. I smiled at him and put my sword down.

"Well, it's easy when I can smell you enter the room "I chuckled

"That would be the smell of a man." he joked. "We missed you in training today."

"I just haven't been up to it." I lied. I had developed some feelings for Hendriick recently. It has become harder to train with him. He was too much of a distraction for me. I knew it would never happen. No one wanted to be seen with a princess with a scar across her face.

"You're going to lose your touch if you don't practice princess." he said as he put his sword back in its holster.

"How will I lose my touch if I have you sneaking up on me all the time to test me?"

"You're right Princess." he smiled. "What are you doing alone in your room? Fantasizing of the outside world again?" He knew me too well.

"Hendriick what's it like? You get to leave as you please and I'm stuck here." I asked eagerly to know. I sat down on my bed and waited for his response.

"And yet they would trade places with you in a heartbeat." he pointed out.

"I do not see a problem with that."

"Oh, but I do. Your father is King." he reminded me.

"Ugh, don't remind me." I stood back up and walked back to my window. The sun had finally rested behind the mountain and the moon began to rise in its place. "I just want to go there. At least once. I hate being a prisoner here."

"Jacintha, you are no prisoner. You are free to go as you please. If it is in the castle walls."

"That's the problem Hendriick. I have lived my whole life in these walls, and I don't want to die with not seeing what's beyond them." I turned to face him. "Please Hendriick, will you take me to Rosewich." I begged him.

"And disobey my lord?" he replied "I'm sorry Jacintha. The King will have my head."

"Not if he doesn't know." I said with a smirk.

"I don't like that look."

"Oh, come on Hendriick. He will not find out. Not if we plan it right. I promise I won't be gone all night, and no one will know."

"I don't know princess."

"Oh, please, please, please. I beg of you. Just one time and I promise to never ask anything of you ever again." I begged once more.

"Alright but, you have to help me train the future knights every day."

I jumped up and screamed with excitement like I was a little girl again. "I will. I promise." I jumped in Hendrick's arms and wrapped my arms around him and kissed his cheek. Hendriick froze from shock. He never expected me to do that, and I could tell by how red his face was that he didn't mind it either. "Thank you so much Hendriick. What time are we going? Shall I get ready now?"

"Calm down princess. We will not be going tonight." He pulled back from me, and my smile quickly vanished. "If we're going to do this only once then we're going to go when the village has their festivities."

"When will that be." I pouted.

"I'm not sure yet but, I will find out. Until then, you will report to me every day at sunrise to train."

. That didn't seem fair to me to have to train when I hadn't gotten what I wanted yet. But I gave him a smile for agreement.

"You don't look so happy for a princess that is getting what she's dreamed about for so long "

"I am so happy. I just hope it's soon "I told him. My face began to hurt from smiling so much. That had never happened before. I tried to wipe the smile away, but I just couldn't.

"It will be." He said before turning to walk out the door. I blushed a little. I was always fond of Hendriick. He always saw the beauty in me and not the princess with a scar on her face.

I remembered something and started to panic. "Hendriick!" I called him before he could exit my room. He turned to look at me and saw the horrid look on my face.

"What is it princess? Are you all, right?" he asked with concern.

"What about my scar? What if I scare them all?" My voice trembled with worry.

He walked up to me and lifted my chin up with his finger. "Princess Jacintha, you are one beauty. Don't ever think you are not." He ran his finger across my scar, and I smiled up at him. "This mark does not define who you are in here" he pointed to my heart.

"Thank you Hendriick for everything." I said with a big smile on my face. I wanted to kiss him again but this time on his lips, but I grew too nervous. I didn't want to spring too much on him at once.

"There's that beautiful smile." He spoke. "I must go now, princess. We will talk soon."

I jumped on my bed on my back with my arms spread out after he left. My heart was full of excitement. I had to come up with a plan to sneak out without my father or sister knowing about it. The last thing I didn't want was for Hendriick to get in trouble for helping me. The thought of being able to leave this place, even for just one night, was a dream come true. Hendriick being by my side was icing on the cake. Not only did I get a night out, but I got a night out with my crush. Our relationship could blossom into something beautiful. The more I thought about it the more I just wanted to scream with excitement.

Chapter Three

Here I was keeping my promise to Hendriick and training every day. It seemed like weeks have passed and he had not even mentioned going to Rosewich. I was frustrated and I took it out on the knight I was training with. I didn't know his name, nor did I care too. He was overly aggressive and didn't hold back despite me being a girl. I was just as aggressive as he and was determined to beat him. I'm not sure when it was that we stopped practicing and got serious but we both had rage in our eyes. He was just showing off to his friends. Or he was giving me all he had, and I wasn't giving up that easily. I'm sure it wasn't easy for a knight to get beat by a girl.

Jacintha" I heard my name being called. I turned my head to look and within seconds I was on my back on the ground. The knight was standing over me with his sword pointed at my neck. He had this disgusting grin on his face. He was proud to have taken victory over me. I heard knights in the background clapping and cheering him on. I was unaware we had an audience.

"Let her up." I heard Hendriick demand. The knight put his sword away without hesitation and reached for my hand to pull me to my feet.

"That was fun Princess." the knight said with a smirk.

I felt disgusted. He put his right hand out to shake mine, but I acted as if I did not notice him and instead turned to look at Hendriick as he approached us. He noticed my angry stare and his half smile vanished instantly. He then looked at the boy and nodded his head at him. The boy knew he was being dismissed. He turned and walked away quickly with no response.

"Jacintha are you okay?" I heard Aletta say. She was running towards us with a worried look on her face.

"You distracted me." I scolded her. "I could have beat him."

"I'm so sorry sister. I did not mean to."

"Distractions will always come; you have to remain focused in battle." Hendriick said.

"This is ridiculous. When will I ever be in battle when I can't even go beyond the castle walls?" I said angrily as I turned away from them both. I began to walk off when Hendriick put his hand on my shoulder to stop me.

"Princess, are you upset with me?" he asked curiously.

"Of course, I'm upset. I kept my promise, and you did not." I scolded him.

"What promise?" asked Aletta as she walked up to us. She walked up wearing a byrnie. I chuckled at how hideous she looked. She rarely came to training so seeing her nit in a dress made me laugh.

"Don't you have a dress or something to try on?" I asked sarcastically.

"I just wanted to see if you wanted to go hang out by the waterfall with me like old times." She said as she put her head down.

"The last time we went to the waterfall together you gave me a scar." I said angrily as I pointed at my face to remind her.

"It was not on purpose Jacintha. I swear I didn't mean for that to happen." she cried out. "When will you forgive me? We were just kids, and I didn't know it would hurt you. I swear Jacintha."

"When you're dead!" I said without thinking.

Aleeta ran away in tears. I just smirked at her. Her tears meant nothing to me.

"Jacintha, that is your sister!" Hendriick scolded me. Aletta busted out in tears and ran off towards the direction of the waterfall.

"I don't care!" I hated her for what she had done to me. No one seemed to understand why I couldn't forgive her.

"I have never seen you like this princess. What has come over you?" Hendriick looked at me like he didn't know me.

"I kept my word, now you keep yours." I told him. I couldn't hold my tongue any longer. Crush or not. He wasn't going to lie to me and get away with it. I wanted what I was promised.

"I will. Just give me a couple more days. Please." He begged.

"A couple more days I'll give but, if you are not ready, I'm going alone." I told him.

"I give you my word princess. Just a couple more days."

I didn't know whether or not I should believe him or not. He has kept me waiting this long already. I decided to give him one more chance. "You have just that." I told him and walked away from him.

Chapter Four

Later that evening I was preparing myself for dinner with my father and sister. Something I grew to hate. Eating with two people I despised as we chatted about our day of doing nothing exciting.

Hendriick barged through my door without even knocking and startled me. "Princess, I have good news." He said to me. "Rosewich is having festivities tomorrow at sundown."

"Maybe next time knock first," luckily, I had just finished changing into my dinner ware.

"I am so sorry princess," he begged for forgiveness.

"You are forgiven." I told him before going through the dresses I had on hand. I was excited but still angry with him. "Finally. What shall I wear?" I asked him.

"Try not to dress like a princess. The peasants seem too not like the rich very much."

"I am not Aletta; I have a black gown with a hood to help cover my face." I told him.

"That will work I suppose."

"Have you figured out how we will get passed the guards at the entrance?"

"Yes, there are several swords that need to be taken to the blacksmith to be fixed. You will hide in the wagon with those said swords as I leave for Rosewich."

"If I get caught, I will assure my father you had nothing to do with me leaving."

"I hope you are ready for this adventure."

"I have been planning this for years Hendriick." O smirked at him. "Did you underestimate me?"

"Not at all princess. It was you who underestimated me." His half smile made butterflies dance in my stomach. Something I was not used to at all.

A knock on my door startled us both. Aletta walked in wearing her new fancy pink gown and her curly locks were pinned back.

"Father sent me to call upon you Jacinta. He wishes you to join us for dinner." she said. "Hello Hendriick."

"Don't I join him for dinner every night?" I uttered under my breath.

"Good evening princess Aletta. You are looking incredibly beautiful this evening." He grabbed her hand and kissed it. I rolled my eyes but neither noticed.

"Thank you Hendriick." She giggled like a child.

"Tell father I will be right there." I interrupted before they made me sick.

"I will sister. See you soon." Aletta said before she left the room.

"I better go princess. I will see you tomorrow morning at sunrise for training."

"Don't remind me." I said sarcastically

Hendriick chuckled before heading for the door.

"Thanks again Hendriick. I can't wait."

"It's my pleasure princess. Enjoy dinner with the king and princess Aleeta." It is going to be a momentous day tomorrow."

"I will certainly try." I assured him.

Dinner was like every other night. Father asking us how our days went. We would have to lie and tell him all the exciting things we did even though they weren't exciting. He didn't like it when I brought up going on adventures. Or even going with him to pick up supplies.

"It's too dangerous for a princess outside these walls." he would say.

No one has ever attacked our Kingdom since we built it. If they had, he never told us about it. I think he enjoyed us living in fear from the outside world.

After dinner I ran up the million stairs back to my room. I had to find something perfect to wear. Too bad I didn't know any of Aleeta's tailor's. They would know exactly what I should wear. It has been years since I've seen anyone come through the gates of Dateron. My father was very strict. No outsiders were allowed unless it was a serious matter. Even then my father would lock us in our rooms with multiple guards protecting us from something that could happen.

I wondered if the people in the village would accept me for what I looked like. I began to fantasize about Rosewich like a did a million times before. I could imagine a lot of happy faces and I bet the people were very friendly to one another. I can picture everyone dancing and laughing and having an enjoyable time. I almost couldn't sleep just thinking about it all. I was so happy to break free of these castle walls even if it was only for a night.

Chapter Five

I wore a plain black dress. Nothing fancy like Aletta would wear. I had a hooded black overcoat so no one would think it was me sneaking out. I was headed down the stairs and, on my way to meet Hendriick when my father's voice stopped me.

"Jacintha. Where are you going?" he asked firmly. I turned to face him, and he stood still at the top of the staircase.

I froze. I had to think of something quick before he suspected something and crushed my dreams forever. "I'm going to the waterfall." I blurted it out without thinking it through.

"I thought you hated the waterfall?" he asked, staring at me like he knew I was lying to him.

"You always taught us to face our fears father. Maybe it's time that I do." I told him.

"Maybe it's time that you forgive your sister as well Jacintha. You have made her suffer long enough. She is trying hard to get you to forgive her."

"I can't forgive her right now father. What she did to me," I took a deep breath. "I will suffer for the rest of my life."

"You can't live with hate in your heart Jacintha. Your mother taught me that."

"I don't want to talk about mother, father."

"I understand Jacintha. I know one day you will and just know I'll be here when you are ready."

"Okay father. I will remember that. I must go now." I didn't want to seem too desperate to leave.

"Be careful Jacintha." He yelled at me as I continued down the stairs.

"I will father." I yelled back at him.

Hendriick already had everything ready to go by the time I reached him.

"Where have you been?" He sounded upset. "You are late!"

"My father saw me." I told him as I climbed into the back of the wagon. Hendriick had a scared look on his face while he looked in all directions for the king. "Relax Hendriick. He is not following me." I assured him.

"What did you tell him?" he asked curiously.

"That I was going to go face my fears." I giggled. I still couldn't believe my father fell for that.

"Face your fears? Really? I suppose you are going to be doing quite the opposite." He laughed.

"Yes, I will if you hurry up so we can go." I told him.

"Yes, of course princess." He quickly jumped on his stallion, and we were off to the entrance of the castle. I quickly hid underneath the tarp where I couldn't be seen. We came to a complete stop. Hendriick must have been talking with the guards about something because we were stopped longer than I imagined. I couldn't make out anything they were saying, I just heard mumbles and a few laughs in between. I laid there quietly trying not to move. I was starting to get impatient when we began to move again. I let out a sigh. I was finally beyond the castle walls. I peeked out the back of the wagon and the castle grew smaller and smaller as we got farther away. I stayed still until Hendriick told me the coast was clear. He helped me out of the wagon and pointed to Rosewich.

Chapter Six

"There it is princess. What you have been waiting to see." Hendriick said as he gazed at the village with a smile on his face.

I didn't respond.

My anticipation slowly vanished the closer we got. It looked smaller than I imagined it had been. As we approached Rosewich grounds the first thing I noticed were the many different shops made of stone. A dirt road was in between the shops. People were scattered all around. We had to move slowly to get through the dozens of people.

I noticed a tailor shop. They had dresses on display in front of their shop. They looked nothing like the dresses Aleeta wore. These were raggedy. Not nearly as pretty as Aleeta's. I assumed there was more than one tailor around.

I saw the iron worker's standing around laughing amongst each other. Markets with fresh vegetables laid out on display with people filling their bags. Kids ran around unattended. Is this what freedom was like? Were they living the dream?

We came to a stop and Hendriick jumped off his horse. He then helped me down.

"Why are we stopping?" I was starting to panic.

Hendriick chuckled at the sight of me. "This is the middle of town. Didn't you want to laugh and dance?" He pointed in front of us. I hadn't noticed it before, but several fires lit up the village.

Right in the center of town there was a really big bon fire. People had metal cups drinking, laughing, singing. I heard music being played in the distance.

"What do I do?" I asked confused.

"You go live your dream and I'm going to drop these swords off to be fixed."

"You can't just leave me here?" I grabbed Hendriick's arm and squeezed it tight.

Hendriick laughed. "I won't be long I promise. I'll be back before you even notice that I am gone."

"Okay," I said still hesitant.

I didn't want to be left here but I guess I really didn't have a choice in the matter. I watched Hendriick walk away from me. He was a friendly person it seemed. He always looked intimidating to me. Of course, I've trained with him for years, so I guess that only makes sense. I was seeing a different side of him. His weakness maybe? I didn't like it. I wasn't sure I liked Rosewich either. It wasn't like I imagined at all. I looked at my surroundings again, it was filthy. Women dressed in rags. The men still had dirty faces and looked sweaty. The children even looked dirty, and their parents didn't seem to care. How could they live in this filth? Did this lifestyle make them happy?

My hood still covered my face as I walked towards the area where everyone was dancing. I figured I must try to enjoy myself while Hendriick was gone. I felt something pulling at my dress. I stopped and I looked down and saw a little boy standing beside me. His face was dirty like he had just eaten some berries. At least I hoped it was berries.

"What do you want?" I looked at him confused.

He didn't say a word to me. Instead, he held out his hand.

"What is it that you want boy?" I asked again only this time sterner. Did these children have no manners? He just stood there with his hand out. I was beginning to get frustrated, so I decided to just ignore him.

I began to walk away when I felt another tug on my dress. I looked down once more and it was the same dirty little boy.

"What in the world do you want child?" I asked him.

Again, he just stood there with his hand out.

"He wants to dance with you miss." an overweight woman said to me as she strolled by us turning in circles.

I looked at the boy again. "Is that what you want?"

He nodded his head up and down and smiled really big. His teeth were just as dirty as his face. I think he had a few missing as well.

"Oh, what the hell," I said under my breath. I grabbed the boys dirty hand and let him lead me to where everyone was dancing.

I didn't know how to dance, and I kept stepping on the little boys' toes. I almost felt bad for him but every time I glanced down to look at him, he had a big smile on his face. I looked around for Hendriick but I did not see him. I can't believe he is taking so long. He will be scolded for this.

The little boy stopped moving and I heard him gasp. I looked down at him and his face was almost pale. Like he had just seen a ghost. He was terrified.

"What is it?" I asked frantically.

He didn't say anything. He just kept staring at me. I felt my face and realized that my hood came off. It must have been when he spun me around. It's my face that he was frightened of. Seeing my face made him so scared.

"Why you're no lady, you're a witch." he said before slowly backing away from me, he then started screaming, "She's a witch!" everyone around me gasped. Women were grabbing their children and holding them close. Fear was plastered across their faces. The music stopped and everyone was staring at me, frightened.

"I'm not a witch." I cried out scared and alone.

"Hang her! Before she hurts our children." I heard a woman yell out. I looked around for Hendriick again and still no sight of him.

"I am Princess Jacintha, Daughter of King Kornel. I am not a witch!" I said as my voice trembled with fear. Men were walking towards me slowly from all angles. I tried to run but one of them grabbed my arm tightly to where I couldn't move.

"The king only has one daughter, and her name is Aletta." he said to me.

"No!" I shook my head. I was horrified. "Ask Hendriick." I begged them. By then I felt myself being lifted in the air and carried away. I tried my hardest to break free, but they were holding me too tight.

"Throw her in the fire!" several people shouted.

"We have a better plan," One of the guys carrying me yelled back.

"HENDRIICK! HENDRIICK HELP ME!" I cried out. "Let me down. I am not a witch!" I begged them but they wouldn't listen to me. They ignored me. Just like Hendriick was doing. Was this his plan all along? Did he set me up to be killed? My father would have his head when he finds out about this.

My body was shaking with fear. What were they going to do to me? This wasn't a dream. This was a nightmare. I needed to get away, but I was helpless. All that training for nothing. I wasn't prepared for this. My father was right about these peasants.

"We're going to teach you a lesson. Don't ever come back to Rosewich again witch!" I heard one of the men say. It was dark and I couldn't see anything except a flame from the stick one of the guys had leading the way. We finally came to a stop, and they let me down.

"Please don't hurt me!" I begged them. I could barely see their faces. We were away from the village. It was darker. Only three torches lit up the surroundings and I still could barely see a thing.

They dropped me on the ground, and I landed on my arm. I cried out in pain. I was freezing and hurt. In more ways than one.

Too late witch!" a man said and then he pushed me. I felt myself falling. My heart was jumping, and my stomach was turning. I fell into the water and my body was stung. I couldn't breathe. I could barely move. I didn't know how to swim. I just kept sinking deeper and deeper. My dream turned into a nightmare. I felt like I did when Aleeta pushed me down the waterfall. Only this time it was a cliff, I think. I could only see darkness. People cheered as I screamed my lungs out. My body stung as soon as I hit that water. I had a flashback to when I was little, and Aleeta had pushed me. I closed my eyes tight as I started to sink farther down. I knew no one was going to save me this time. I made a mistake. I should have never come here.

I felt something grab me. I didn't dare open my eyes. Before I knew it, I was above water and took a big gasp of air. I was then pulled ashore. I couldn't see my savior due to the darkness. Was it Hendriick? Did he come back to save me? I just sat there soaked and freezing, still coughing up water and trying to breathe. I was thankful for being alive. I was thankful for this person for saving my life.

Chapter Seven

"Are you okay?" asked the mysterious man.

"No! I'm not. Why did those peasants do that to me? They tried to kill me." I answered angrily.

"They were frightened." He defended them. "They didn't know who you were."

"They were frightened. I was the one thrown off a cliff." I said rudely.

"I am sorry. You did not deserve that." he said sincerely. "My name is Jaxon. What is your name?"

"I am Princess Jacintha, daughter of King Kornel."

"Are you really a Princess?" he asked in disbelief.

"Of course, I am. Why would I lie about something like that?"

"It's just that." he hesitated. "Never mind."

I was going to say something rude, but something stole my attention. I saw flames in the distance. "They are coming to finish me off." I cried out as I panicked.

"I won't let that happen. I promise you that princess." We both stood to our feet quickly. My dress was soaked with water and the sand from the shore grew attached to me as well.

THE FALL OF JACINTHA

As the flames grew closer, I hid behind Jaxon. There were several men carrying torches and some on horses. My body started to shiver. Not only was I scared but I was freezing cold as well.

"Jacintha!" I heard a familiar voice call out my name.

"Father!" I pushed Jaxon out of my way and ran towards my father's voice.

"Princess wait!" Jaxon called out to me. I ignored him and kept running. I was relieved to hear my father's voice. When I finally approached my father, he had jumped off his horse that was leading the knights.

He hugged me tightly. "I have been looking everywhere for you." I could hear the trembling in his voice, he was scared.

"I'm sorry father. I promise I will never disobey you again." I didn't let go of him. His body was warm, and my father had never shown me such emotions before.

"Princess!" I heard Jaxon running up from behind me. My father pulled me behind him.

"Who are you, and what did you do to my daughter?" he demanded to know.

"I'm Jaxon. I saved your daughter from drowning." he replied.

"I am your king! You kneel before me before you speak!"

"I'm so sorry my lord." Jaxon kneeled at once.

"Yes father. The people of Rosewich called me a witch and threw me off the cliff into the water. Jaxon pulled me out and saved my life." I told him with tears in my eyes.

"I told you Jacintha to never come here. My fears were right. You could have died." he scolded me. But I could tell he was scared too. His words trembled.

"I know father. I am terribly sorry." I lowered my head in shame.

"You saved my daughter's life Jaxon. I am forever in your debt. Will you come back to Dateron with us? There I can try to repay you for such gratitude and heroism."

"It would be my honor, King Kornel." Jaxon accepted. "I must do some things here before I leave. Will the invitation still stand tomorrow?"

"Yes, it will." my father told him.

I rode with my father on the back of his horse on the journey back to Dateron. We didn't speak a word. When we returned to the castle I went straight to my room. I still didn't know where Hendriick disappeared to. When I found him, he was going to regret ever leaving me like that.

Chapter Eight

"Time to get up. We are having a guest today. Also, father wishes to speak with you." Aletta came barging in my room and went straight to the curtains to open them. The sun's rays hit my face vigorously. I tried to cover my face with my blanket, but she just peeled them from me.

"What is your problem?" I demanded to know.

"Father said he needed to speak with you and to not let you go back to sleep." she replied, "I'm doing as our king as asked. Unlike some."

"Oh, so you heard about me sneaking out?" That was a dumb question. Of course, she did. She knew all the gossip in the castle and some from Rosewich.

"Of course, I have. If it wasn't for Hendriick," she began to say. "Who knows what could have happened to you Jacintha."

"Hendriick?" I said without hiding how angry I was.

"Yes Hendriick. He told father that he saw you sneaking out and he was terrified something would happen to you."

I couldn't believe it. Hendriick betrayed me. That's why I couldn't find him. He left me to go tell my father where I was. I was so angry. I wanted to destroy him for betraying me.

"Where is he?" I asked. "Where can I find Hendriick?"

"I do not know at this very second but, what I do know is that you better go find father before he finds you."

"Fine. I'll deal with Hendriick later." I told her.

"He was just looking out for you Jacintha. Why are you so angry?"

"You wouldn't understand Aletta. Now leave my room at once so I can get dressed and find father."

"As you wish sister." She didn't hesitate and quickly left. I didn't want to face my father. I knew he was going to punish me, and I was too tired to deal with the consequences.

I found my father sitting on his throne with Hendriick standing by his side. He was in his knight armor. As I approached my father, I noticed his eyes were locked on me. Shivers went down my spine.

"Hendriick, you can leave." My father said without taking his eyes off me. Hendriick bowed his head at my father and walked away without even acknowledging me. It was like I wasn't even there. He betrayed me. Why did he get to act like I did something to him? I'm the one who almost died. I could feel my temperature rising and I was getting angry. I turned to say something to him. I was going to tell him off.

"Jacintha!" my father yelled my name before I could even get a word out. I quickly turned to face him and once again his eyes were locked with mine, his stare was so cold. "You will not speak nor seek revenge on Hendriick. Do you understand?" he ordered.

"But." was all I could say before he interrupted me.

"No but Jacintha, this is a command. You will do as I say. I'm demanding this as your king and as your father. If you choose to disobey me, proper punishment will be brought upon you.

"I don't understand why he isn't being punished for leaving me there. I was almost killed by these peasants, and he ran away." I said angrily.

"He left long before there was any threat towards you. He told me your plans for going to Rosewich in advance. I told him to follow through with your plans to teach you a lesson."

I couldn't believe that I was set up like this. I felt sick to my stomach. "So, your plan was to get rid of me for good? No one believed I was your daughter. They have only heard about Aletta but not I. Am I that much of a disgrace to you father that you would help Hendriick set me up to be killed?" My blood was boiling.

"That is enough!" he yelled at me. "I did not know they were going to try to hurt you. I wanted you to experience what you have been dreaming about. Hendriick explained to me how your face lit up every time you talked about leaving this castle. The castle I built for you and your sister to keep you safe. He said you felt like a prisoner here. Do you know how much that hurt me to hear Jacintha?"

"I'm sorry father." I didn't know what else to say to him. I put my head down with shame. I couldn't dare look him in the eyes after what he just said.

"Had I known these peasants would throw you off a cliff, Hendriick would not have left you. I would have never allowed such a repugnant act towards my own child. I am your father Jacintha and you and your sister's protection is my main goal in life. You wanted an adventure and now you know what peasants are like beyond these castle walls. I am sorry that this happened to you again Jacintha, but I also hope it has taught you something."

"Yes, father it has." It has taught me to never trust anyone ever again.

"Hendriick cares about you Jacintha and he was only looking out for you. I hope that you forgive him as I have forgiven you."

There was no way I could forgive Hendriick for his betrayal. I always thought that one day we would be more than friends but, that friendship died when I went over that cliff. "I have a question father."

"What is it?"

"You never said as to why the peasants of Rosewich did not know who I was. Why don't they?" I dared to ask the question he previously avoided answering.

"Jacintha, you hold a secret only you and I know about. If that secret is ever revealed I cannot protect you."

"So, if the secret is revealed you want to act as if I am not your daughter?" I crossed my arms and gave him the cold stare he gave me earlier. "Maybe I should tell everyone myself and let it be known what I did, I did it for you."

"Jacintha please. Let it go. Think about Aletta. It could break her heart to know the truth and it could mess up her future as to ruling this, Kingdom."

"Aletta? Why does everything always come down to Aletta? Look what she did to me!" I pointed at my scar. "I was claimed to be a witch because of her. I got thrown off a cliff because of her. I have suffered enough because of her. Yet, you still speak of me as the ill one. she is your golden child while I'll always remain the daughter you hide from the world because of what she did to me." I didn't realize how loud my voice was, nor did I notice I was crying.

"Jacintha, that is not true." he said sincerely.

"Yes, it is father, and you know it!" I didn't give him time to respond. Instead, I ran from him and returned to my room. I lay in my bed crying. He was still holding that secret against me. He knew I did that for him and yet, he was still punishing me for it.

Chapter Nine

A knock on my door startled me as I was getting dressed for dinner with Jaxon. Of course, my father and sister would be there as well, even though I wished they wouldn't. "Come in." I yelled towards the door. To my surprise it was Hendriick. I grew upset quickly. "What are you doing here? Did my father send you here?" He could tell I was angry. I wasn't going to let him think I was anything but that.

"I know you're angry with me." he began to say.

"That's an understatement." I interrupted him.

"I do not deserve your forgiveness Jacintha but, I am hoping one day you will. I care for you deeply and I now regret ever telling the king. I should have been there to protect you." he confessed.

"Yes, you should have. I cannot and will not forgive you. You betrayed me Hendriick and if it were up to me, you would be punished for that betrayal."

"You don't really mean that, do you, Jacintha?" he asked in disbelief.

"Of course, I mean it." I turned away from him. I couldn't stand to look at his face any longer.

"Do you no longer feel what you have felt for me all these years?" He placed his hand on my shoulder. I quickly moved away from him.

"My feelings for you Hendriick, died when I was thrown off that cliff." I told him. His eyes looked as if I had just broken his heart but, it was my heart that was broken. It was I who he had betrayed.

"I understand." he put his head down. I was a little disappointed he didn't try to convince me or even shed a tear. He just took a couple steps back from me and stood straight up as if we were never anything.

"Is there a reason you are still standing in my room?" I asked rudely.

"The king has asked me to escort you to dinner. Jaxon has arrived and Aletta is keeping him company as they wait for your presence." he answered without even looking at me.

"I do not need an escort and if I did, it would be someone of my choosing and not you."

"As you wish Princess." He then left. I was still upset. I didn't think he would give in so easily. I might have forgiven him if he tried. I was more upset with my father for sending him to fetch me after he commanded me to never speak to him again.

Jaxon was the first person to greet me when I walked into the dining room. My heart skipped a beat. Butterflies went wild in my stomach. He was gorgeous. Jaw dropping handsome. His hair was long, black, and pulled back. His brown eyes sparkled and hypnotized me at first glance. His smile made me melt and he had luscious lips I wanted to kiss right away. His perfect muscular body proved he wasn't like those other peasants who looked as if they were lazy. Jaxon was a real man. A man I could see myself marrying and having a family with. A man that could one day rule Dateron by my side. He spoke to me, but I didn't hear him. I was still fantasizing about our future together.

"Jacintha don't be rude. Shake the man's hand." My father's barbarous voice snapped me back into reality.

"I am so sorry Jaxon." I apologized to him as I blushed. I grabbed his hand to shake it. His hand felt rough. From all the real man work he does.

"Not a problem Jacintha. How have you been doing?" he asked.

"I am still distraught with everything that has happened. I've never been so frightened in my life before. I don't know how I could ever repay you for saving my life." I told him.

"You owe me nothing Jacintha. You have all showed me much gratitude by just inviting me here today." He held my hand and led me to my seat. He pulled out my chair for me to sit and pushed it in. I was blushing so hard. My father sat at the head of the table. I was sitting on his right side where I always sat and Aletta across from me on his left. She was dressed in a sparkling white dress. I didn't recognize it so father must have bought her a new one just for the occasion. Jaxon took the seat beside me which made me nervous. I never had these feelings before, not even with Hendriick. I always thought Hendriick and I would one day marry. I figured he would love me one day more than loving serving my father. I'm glad he showed me his betrayal now. Better now than when we were married.

"We just want to thank you Jaxon for saving Jacintha. You showed such bravery. We couldn't bare it if we had lost her." Aletta said with a smile.

They couldn't bear it? Yeah right! I rolled my eyes at her fakeness.

"I would have done it for anyone. She did not deserve what was done to her." He looked at me and smiled.

"She isn't just anyone. She is a princess, and she is special to us. Don't you agree father?" We all looked to my father for his response.

"You are in fact right Aletta. Jacintha is particularly important to our family, and we love her very much." My father looked at me and smiled. I didn't know if he was putting on an act because we had a guest or if he was being sincere.

"I'm glad I could help." Jaxon said.

"So, tell us about yourself Jaxon." Aletta asked.

"What would you like to know?"

"Well for starters, when did you become a hero?" she asked flirtatiously.

Jaxon blushed at Aletta's question. "I'm no hero."

"You are my hero Jaxon." I blurted out. Everyone turned their heads to look at me.

"Thank you, Jacintha." He seemed nervous. "When I was ten, I lost both my parents. I had to take care of myself until I was twelve. That is when I met Mazelina. She raised me from then and taught me how to do a lot of things. She passed on a couple of years ago. I came to Rosewich shortly after that. It wasn't hard to find work and that's what I have been doing every day since. I usually do not take part in the town's festivities but when I was dropping off some wood, I saw what they were doing to Jacintha. I knew I had to save her." None of us was expecting a story like that from him. My eyes watered up hearing what happened to him. Growing up having to take care of himself like that, then the only person to help you dies too.

"And we will forever be grateful to you." Aletta broke the awkward silence. "We have something in common. We lost our mother as well at an early age."

"Aletta!" Our father interrupted her.

"I am sorry for your family's loss. It is not easy losing a loved one.

"My apologies Jaxon. Speaking of my queen, Tianna, is something I cannot do, even to this day." father told him. He looked at me with that cold look again. I looked away from him and planned to ignore him the rest of the night.

"I know my life is very different from living in a castle and having everything but, that life made me who I am today." Jaxon said out of nowhere.

"Trust me Jaxon. It's not all it is cut out to be." I told him.

"Jacintha!" I looked back at my father who was staring back at me with a disapproving look on his face.

"Where do you live now?" Aletta asked all cheery.

"In the woods." he replied.

"Oh no you unfortunate thing." before anyone could say anything else Hendriick walked in interrupting our dinner. He whispered something in my father's ears.

My father stood up from his seat. "My apologies, I need to excuse myself."

"Father before you go, can I make a request?" I asked.

"Of course, Jacintha."

"Is it possible that Jaxon can stay in one of the many spare rooms we have?" I looked at Hendriick for a reaction but nothing.

"Oh, please father?" Aletta sounded excited.

"Oh no, I could not intrude like that."

"You saved my life Jaxon. Any other person who has just left me to drown." I said still staring at Hendriick. He still ignored me.

"Yes, he can and Jaxon we will not take no for an answer. You can stay if you see fit. When you are done with dinner Hendriick will see you to your room."

"Yes, my lord." Hendriick said to him.

"I cannot thank you all enough."

"Thank you, father, for your kind generosity." I told him.

"Jacintha, Aletta, Jaxon, I must leave now. I will see you all later."

We continued our dinner without father present. The more Jaxon told us about himself the more I fell for him. He has been to a lot of places, and he assured me not everyone was like the peasants in Rosewich. I felt a lot safer knowing he would be staying in the castle, and I would get to see him every day. I was determined to marry this man.

Chapter Ten

Weeks had gone by, and I felt happier. Everyone noticed my change in mood, and they became pleasant to be around. I knew Jaxon was the only reason I was smiling and giddy. We were growing closer. I knew he felt the same for me. I could see it in his eyes.

I sat on Aleeta's bed braiding her hair. Since Jaxon has been here, he has encouraged me to forgive Aleeta for what she did to me as a child. Besides, I had a favor to ask of her and I was trying to get the courage to ask.

"I need a dress," I finally just blurted it out.

Aleeta turned to look at me with a shocked expression. "Are you being serious?" she finally spoke.

"Yes, I'm being serious." I hated to admit it. The last thing o wanted was the million questions I knew Aleeta was about to ask. I didn't know the tailor's personally like she did. So, I had no choice but to ask her.

"Who is it for?" her face lit up with excitement.

"It's for me," I sarcastically said.

"But who is he that has made our Jacintha want to be normal?"

"Normal?" I rolled my eyes. "No one. I just wanted to try something nicer."

"You have been a lot nicer lately Jacintha." she smiled. "I've heard chatter around the castle, and they say you have become more pleasant to be around."

"Does it look like I care what people say about me?" I snapped. I was getting impatient waiting for an answer.

My anger didn't faze Aleeta one bit. She continued to wear that ridiculous smile. "How soon do you need it?"

"Tonight!"

"That is very short notice Jacintha."

"Well how long does it take?"

"At least a week."

"I can't wait that long." I uttered.

"I have the perfect dress for you," Aleeta jumped up and down with excitement.

"I don't want to wear something you've already worn."

"I haven't worn this dress yet. But it is beautiful. I just know you would love it."

"Well, where is it?" I looked around her room waiting for her to show me the dress, but she just stood there.

"It's not here. I'll have to go get it."

"What are you waiting for?"

Aleeta giggled. "Calm down sister. I will have it ready for you tonight. Don't be so anxious."

I couldn't help but be anxious. I wanted everything to be perfect when I confessed my love to Jaxon. This was a big deal to me. He saved my life, and I knew I would be the perfect wife to him. I was forever in his debt.

"Come back in a few hours and I will have everything ready for you. I will even do your hair and anything else you want."

"I will do so,"

For the first time I felt butterflies in my stomach. I was the happiest I had ever been. Once Jaxon agreed to spend his life with me, I knew I would always be happy.

I left my sister's room and returned to mine. I laid in my bed just fantasizing about the life I was about to have. I was going to be married soon and have my own family. Jaxon was going to take me far away to a new life. The life I truly deserved.

Chapter Eleven

I was headed to Aletta's room to get the dress she said she would have ready for me. I felt a little nervous. I guess I had every right to be. Tonight, my whole world was going to change. That was scary and exciting at the same time. I was ready for the change.

When I approached Aleeta's door, I heard her talking to someone. A man. Did I just catch Aleeta with a man in her room? Father would lose his sanity if he knew about this. I could get her to do anything for me if she wanted me to keep my mouth shut about it. I smirked at the thought of the things I could get her to do. "You can't think like that Jacintha," I said to myself. "Everything is going to change soon."

I slowly cracked the door open and peeked in with one eye. I had to know who she was sneaking around with. My jaw dropped when I saw Aletta with her filthy lips on Jaxon. They were kissing. It felt like a sword just went through my heart. I turned and leaned against the wall. I did not know what had come over me. My knees grew weak. I thought I was going to faint. Breathing became harder. I stood there trying to collect myself.

"You are my heart and soul Aletta." I heard Jaxon say to her.

"As you are mine as well." she said back to him.

My face became hot from the anger I was feeling. I wanted to kill them both. My heart shattered and I could barely breathe. I was not going to let Aletta get away with taking him from me. I kicked the door opened and they both jumped apart.

"Jacintha, what are you doing?" Aletta cried out.

"Does father know about this?" I demanded to know.

"Know about what?" She acted clueless.

"I was just helping her..." Jaxon started to say.

"Do not speak!" I demanded of him, and he did as he was told.

I looked my sister straight in her eyes. "Does father know you claim to be in love with this peasant?"

"You mean the peasant that saved your life?" She defended him. Her stare was just as cold as our father's.

"I saw you kissing him and heard you confessing your love to one another." I said in disgust.

"Jacintha, please do not tell father." she started to beg. I enjoyed the sight of her begging.

"This ends now." I told them.

"I love him Jacintha and he loves me." she began to cry. "You know what that feels like don't you?"

"It is true. She is the soul I have been searching for." Jaxon jumped in.

"Didn't I tell you not to speak?" I snapped at him.

"Jacintha please. I beg of you sister. Do you have no heart?" She had the audacity to ask me that after what she had done to me.

"Not anymore I don't." I told her. I enjoyed watching my sister in pain. Her tears falling like the waterfall, she pushed me down. She deserved every drop. "Say your farewells and I will announce to father that Jaxon will be leaving Dateron by sunset." I stormed out of the room not giving any of them the chance to respond. Aletta's cries grew louder.

I cried on my bed after returning to my room. I loved Jaxon and my sister took him from me. Just like she took my looks and my life. She could have anyone she wanted. Why could she not let me have him? I was the perfect one for him. She couldn't possibly love him more than I did. She used the guys around here to her advantage. She was going to ruin Jaxon and throw him away like she did all the rest. I had to tell my father. I could not bear to see them together.

Chapter Twelve

I went to search for my father to tell him Jaxon was departing Dateron but, to my surprise, I found Aletta and Jaxon already with him. They all looked to be happy with smiles on their faces.

"What is going on?" I demanded to know.

"Jaxon has asked for your sister's hand in marriage, and I have approved." my father replied. Jaxon and Aletta just stared at me with their faces lit up. I felt like I was going to be sick. I wanted to grab my sword and chop her head off.

"Aren't you happy for us sister?" Aletta asked sarcastically. They both knew I was infuriated. She was gloating because she thought she won. She didn't win anything. This was far from over.

"You are going to allow her to marry someone she barely even knows?" I questioned my father.

He looked at me confused. "Jaxon has been helpful in the kingdom and let's not forget the bravery he has showed upon this family by saving you." my father said. He hadn't a clue who Jaxon really was. None of us really did. Yeah, he saved me. What was he doing at the bottom of the cliff anyways?

"It would mean so much to me to have your blessing as well Jacintha." Jaxon interrupted.

"Well, you will not get it." I told him.

"Do not think your blessing is required Jacintha. I will marry Jaxon without it." Aletta said rudely.

"You have Jacintha's blessing, and she will be right by your side Aletta, on your big day. I will assure you of it." my father gave me his cold stare again. He wasn't asking me; he was demanding me to give my blessing. As much as it made me sick to say it or to be a part of it, I knew I didn't have a choice in the matter.

"You have my blessing." I mumbled with my head down.

"Speak up Jacintha." he said.

"I said you have my blessing." I looked up and they were all staring at me. They didn't care to have my blessing. Aletta just wanted to throw her happiness in my face. She got Jaxon and the happy ending that was meant for me while I was still miserable with no one to love me. My father just wanted to punish me for what I did so long ago.

"Good, you can help your sister with the details as you have so much free time on your hands now that you are no longer training with Hendriick." he told me.

"Yes father." I bowed my head to him.

"I cannot wait. We will get started in a couple of days." said a stoked Aletta.

Little did she know she wasn't going to marry Jaxon. I was. He was going to be mine one way or another. I walked away from them before they noticed my tears. I wasn't going to let them see how much pain I was in. I was going to get my revenge on Aleeta.

After everyone went to sleep that night, I crept out of my room and into Aletta's room. I looked at her as she slept. I thought how easy it would be to take her life. I could smother her with a pillow, and no one would even know it was me. What a tragic that would be. The king's breathtaking princess smothered in her sleep. Father would be devastated, and Jaxon wouldn't be getting a fairytale wedding unless he was marrying me. I would get the life I deserved and no longer live in my sister's shadow. It seemed too easy. Instead of ending her life, I did something far worse. Something that will cause her emotional pain and would bring me much satisfaction watching how miserable she would be.

I traced my fingers over the scar she had left me. I've been wanting to leave the same scar on her face. Not now. It would only be obvious it was me. I had to do something that would make her not only look but feel ugly. I smiled deviously when the perfect idea came to mind.

I cut off her hair.

Chapter Thirteen

Adrenaline rushed through my body as I ran out of Aletta's room and back into mine. It made me feel alive for some reason. I heard someone walking down the hall. I peeked out my door and saw a flaming torch grow coming towards me. I started to panic. I hope they didn't see me. I jumped into my bed and pretended I was sleeping. I heard my door squeak as it was being slowly opened. My body started to shake.

"Jacintha." a man's voice whispered in my face. I didn't react. "Jacintha, are you awake?" I recognized the voice the second time. I opened my eyes to see who it was. It was Hendriick. What did he want at this hour? I stretched my arms pretending he had woken me from my slumber. He kneeled at the side of my bed.

"Hendriick, what are you doing here? Is it father? Is he okay?" I acted startled as I sat up in my bed. He grabbed my hands and held them. I didn't pull away from him. It was quite comforting.

"He is fine Jacintha. I wanted to talk to you about something." His voice was shaky. "At this hour? It couldn't wait till morning?" I asked. It must have been important if he couldn't wait till morning. Had something terrible happened? There was no way this could have been about Aleeta. I would have heard her screams once she realized what had happened to her.

"I wanted to wait until all was asleep so we wouldn't get caught talking to each other." he confessed.

"Hendriick, what do you want?" I asked rudely. If something terrible had happened, he sure was dragging it out. Just spit it out already.

"I see how you look at Jaxon. You used to look at me that way." he began to say. "I wish you still looked at me that way." he put his head down.

"What are you talking about Hendriick?" I was confused. I pulled my hands from his. I climbed out of bed, and he stood up standing in front of me.

"I miss us Jacintha."

You have to be kidding me. He misses us? Did he forget that he betrayed me? If it weren't for Jaxon, I would be dead. "There was never an us Hendriick. You trained me and I trusted you and then you lost my trust." I reminded him. To be honest, he hasn't said a word to me since that night. Now all of a sudden, he is in my room confessing his love to me?

"We were more than that Jacintha. We were teammates. Why do you lie to yourself? Do you honestly think Jaxon is going to leave Aletta for you?"

"I am not going to have this conversation with you Hendriick. Jaxon is none of your business." I snapped at him.

"Nor is he yours." he said. "I know you don't want to help plan a wedding that you are jealous of."

"I am not jealous!" I yelled.

"Please keep your voice down. You might wake someone up." he begged me.

"Why are you in my room Hendriick? You obviously want something from me, you haven't spoken a word to me since before Jaxon arrived." Why is he doing this to me now? Why not before Jaxon came along? What has changed now?

"Marry me Jacintha." he kneeled down on one knee.

"You have lost your mind." I burst out laughing. I was not expecting him to ask that but, it was hilarious. The distraught look on his face made me laugh even more.

"This isn't a joke Jacintha. I am really asking you to marry me." his serious expression did not fade away.

"Did you think this through before coming in here? Why would you ever think I would say yes?" I asked him. He was a fool. I knew Aleeta had to be behind this. Maybe even my father. Using Hendriick to distract me while she gets away with my man.

He stood back up. "We both want something and the only way we will get it is if you marry me."

"What is it that we both want?" I stopped laughing. I was curious to know his response.

"To one day rule Dateron." he said seriously.

"What makes you think I want to rule this kingdom with you by my side?"

"If Aletta marries Jaxon, the king will give power to Jaxon but, the king knows me better and I know he will grant me that power before Jaxon."

"But you have to be married to a princess to be able to get the throne." I finished his sentence for him. As clever as that plan was, I didn't want to marry Hendriick. I wanted to marry Jaxon. I wanted to rule Dateron with Jaxon by my side. "I suppose your plan would work but, my father has banned me from speaking to you."

"I can talk to the king. He will listen to me." he assured me. "We can plan our wedding instead of you planning Jaxon and Aletta's and having to be hurt every time you see them together." he said as he wrapped his arms around my waist. He leaned in to kiss me, but I pulled my head back. "What is wrong?" he asked concerned.

"I can't marry you Hendriick." I told him. He let go of my waist and his arms fell to his side.

"Why not?" he asked, saddened by my response.

"I do not love you Hendriick. Once before but not now." I confessed.

"It's not about love Jacintha. It's about one day ruling Dateron," he said. "And who better to do that than you and me?"

"So, you have no feelings for me?" I was right. "Did you ever have feelings for me?" This had nothing to do with love. Hendriick was just trying to use me to get to the throne.

"I'm sorry Jacintha but, no I never have." he admitted.

My heart broke once more. I didn't think that him not loving me would have this much of an effect on me. I didn't feel anything for him like I used to but, the fact that he never did, felt like my heart was being ripped out once again. I always thought he and I had a connection but, once again, I was wrong. Before I could say anything, we heard screams coming from another room. We both looked at each other worried.

"Princess Aletta!" Hendriick yelled her name with a panic and we both ran out of my room and into hers.

When we got to her Jaxon was already holding the sobbing princess.

"What's wrong sister?" I asked pretending to be concerned. I already knew what she was crying about.

My father stumbled in before she could answer. He still looked half asleep but, had his sword in his hand. "Is everything okay? I heard screams." he managed to say as he wiped the sleep from his eyes.

"Someone cut off her hair!" Jaxon exclaimed as he grabbed a fist full of the hair that was lying beside Aletta and lifted it up so we all could see. We all gasped. "Who could have done something so cruel?" he asked.

"Jacintha, did you do this to your sister?" My father was quick to blame me.

I rolled me eyes at him. "How dare you accuse me of something this horrid father." I said, trying not to look guilty.

"Who would just come into her room and do such a thing?" Jaxon asked, looking at me. He knew I was guilty.

"Hendriick entered my room as I was sleeping." I blurted out. The look on Hendriick's face was horrifying. If looks could kill, I would be a dead woman.

Everyone looked at Hendriick. "Is this true Hendriick?" my father asked. Hendriick just stood there, staring at me in disbelief. "You will answer your king this once." my father's voice grew louder.

"Yes, my king but, I would never do such a thing to princess Aletta." he uttered.

"We should believe you, why?" I asked him. "You do have a habit of betrayal." I reminded him.

Hendriick didn't know how to respond. He just stood there staring at me. Waiting for me to confess but I was not going to. If his plans were to only use me for his own selfish reasons, then he was going to be used by me for my own selfish reasons.

Aletta pulled herself from the bed with the help of Jaxon. She didn't say anything to any of us. Her eyes were so puffy and red from crying. She walked straight up to Hendriick and slapped him hard across his face.

I gasped.

I wasn't expecting her to do that. None of us did. Hendriick didn't respond. He just stood there with a red handprint on his right cheek.

"I never thought you would do something like this Hendriick." my father told him. "What would you like me to have done with him Aleeta?"

"Off with his head?" she said with no hesitation.

Hendriick looked at me to save him. I knew he was scared.

"For you hair that grows back?" I giggled. "You don't think that is a bit much?"

Aleeta looked at me. "What would you have done?"

"I mean if your face was cut open yeah, I would say off with his head, but I mean you're still alive and well."

"Stop it! The both of you!" My father shouted. "Aleeta, your sister is right. Your hair will grow back. There is no reason to request his death."

My father agreed with me rarely. I was shocked he did this time. By the look on Hendriick's face, he was relieved that he did.

"Lock him up then," Aleeta said. "Lose the key as well. I never want to see him again."

My father nodded his head and escorted Hendriick out of the room and into the dungeon where he kept the other prisoner's.

"I am sorry that this has happened to you Aletta. If there is anything I can do to comfort you, please do not hesitate to ask." I told her.

"Just leave Jacintha." she said with great sadness.

I didn't question her request. As I walked back to my room, I was shocked that my plan worked. Well, I didn't think Hendriick would be the one taking the fall for it. I was still shocked he didn't defend himself. I wondered if he had something up his sleeve. That was just too easy. I don't know how things would have played out had Hendriick not came into my room tonight.

Chapter Fourteen

I saw Jaxon leaving my sister's room. She must have finally cried herself to sleep. It made me jealous even more. She got to feel his touch. And kiss his lips. I could make him happier than she ever could. He walked by me like I was invisible. That wasn't acceptable.

"Why couldn't you love me?" I blurted out to him with tears slowly draining from my eyes.

He stopped and turned to look at me, but I turned my back to him. "I am sorry Jacintha. I do not feel for you like I feel for Aletta. She is my soulmate, and my life makes a lot of sense when I'm with her." he said to me. I turned to face him, and he could see how broken I was. "I'm sorry that we have hurt you. Those were never our intentions,"

"You didn't even give me a chance." I told him. "You should have just let me drown that night and spared me all this pain." He hugged me tightly. His body was warm. His skin was soft. I wrapped my arms around him, and I felt safe. I felt like nothing could go wrong if I were in his arms.

"You will always have a place in my heart Jacintha. I will never regret saving you that night." he whispered in my ear.

I pulled my face away from his neck and looked him in the eyes. There was no way I could let him go. I grabbed his face with both hands and pulled him closer to me and kissed him. He quickly pushed me away from him. "Stop Jacintha! I love Aletta, not you." He stormed away from me and left me standing there, alone. I dried my eyes with my hands and smiled a devious smile. "If I can't have you Jaxon, neither will Aletta."

Little did he know, I had a surprise for him and Aleeta. They wouldn't get it until after dinner, but it was going to be a gift they would never forget.

During dinner, all Aletta could speak about was the wedding. She wanted this big ceremony with everyone there. It made me sick to my stomach. I lost my appetite, and I mostly just pushed my food back and forth with my fork.

"The tailor is already designing the perfect dress for me." she said happily.

"Any dress would look perfect on you." Jaxon placed his hand on top of Aleeta's hand and smiled. They both stared at each other like they were the only two people at the table. It made my stomach turn.

"What about your hair? How are you going to hide the fact that it's ugly?" I blurted out.

The excitement drained from Aleeta's face. She looked at me before putting her head down.

"That is non sense." Jaxon came to her rescue. "If anything, all that hair did was block your beauty." he told her. The smile plastered across her face indicated those were the magic words.

"Jacintha, leave your sister alone!" My father ordered me.

"I think you should wear mothers' necklace on your wedding day." I suggested to her. "What do you think father?" I looked at my father to see his reaction.

"That would be perfect." Aletta blurted out with excitement. We all looked at father and waited for him to respond. He looked a little hesitant at first.

"That is a wonderful idea. Your mother would have loved for you to wear it." he said looking at Aletta with the biggest smile I ever saw him have.

"I can't wait to wear it. Having a piece of mother there with me on my wedding day will be a dream come true. Thank you so much father and thank you Aletta for suggesting it." She jumped out of her seat and gave father a hug.

"I will get the necklace after dinner for you. You can have your tailor make something that will go beautifully with the necklace." father told her.

"That's a great idea father." she said. "I'm just so excited and I can't wait for this day to come."

"I can't wait either." Jaxon said right before he leaned it to kiss her. I rolled my eyes at the sight of them.

"I think we should invite the people of Rosewich as well." she recommended.

"Have you lost your mind?" I said loudly. "Did you forget they tried to kill me? Or do you even care?" I was furious.

"I know sister, but they are the only family Jaxon has." she responded.

"I don't care. Tell her no father." I looked at my father hoping he would be on my side.

"Jacintha, you have to learn to forgive." Is what he said. He made it seem like what they did didn't almost kill me. Like it was no big deal. How could he forgive them and expect me to?

"Please tell me you are joking. You can't be serious right now father. Forgive them for trying to kill me." I felt my blood starting to boil.

"They did not know who you were Jacintha." he admitted.

"And they still do not." I snapped. "The king only has one daughter?" I could feel my body heating up from the anger. Was my father that embarrassed by me?

"It's okay Aletta. We do not need to invite them if their presence is too upsetting for Jacintha." Jaxon proposed.

"If it's too upsetting for me?" I was infuriated. "Invite whomever you choose. This is your wedding, not mine. I will be no part of it." I stood up from my seat.

"Jacintha, you do not mean what you say. Sit child and we will figure this out as a family." my father said to me.

"I will do no such thing. This hadn't been a family since mother died!" I ran away from the table before anyone could say anything and returned to my room.

I paced back and forth waiting for my father to storm through my room to give me my punishment for not obeying his orders. Then again, he will send Riickard to fetch me seeing how Hendriick no longer can.

My father announced Riickard to take the place of Hendriick just hours after throwing him in a cell. Riickard was the next in line to lead. He was also a lot stricter than Hendriick was. I wouldn't be able to get away with anything. Not that Hendriick let me get away with a whole lot.

I went to go speak with him earlier in the day. I was curious as to know why he would take the fall for something he did not do. He did not wish to speak to me. No surprise there. I will not be going to see him again. Over an hour had passed and no one came to yell at me. I was about to go search for my father when knights barged in my room.

"What in heavens are you doing?" I demanded to know.

"Kings orders." Riickard replied. They scattered around the room searching for something.

"What were his orders?" I demanded to know.

"To find the necklace that belonged to Queen Tianna." he said. I wasn't surprised my father would blame me for that as well.

"Well go ahead and look. You won't find it here." I sat at my window seal watching as they destroyed my room. I didn't care because I knew exactly where the necklace was, and it wasn't in my room nor in my possession. The king entered my room and all the knights stopped what they were doing and bowed to him. I just rolled my eyes.

"Father, why would you send these men to destroy my room."

"Where is it Jacintha? I know you took it."

"You keep accusing me of things father. Why do you think of me as someone that would steal mothers' necklace?"

"Do not act like you are innocent. We both know what you can do."

"Stop making me out to be the bad person when what I did was for you."

"I never told you to do that Jacintha. That is all on you."

"I protected you from a whore, and this is how you repay me?"

My father slapped me hard across the face. Now I know how Hendriick must have felt.

"You will not speak of your mother that way."

"I do not have mother's necklace." I stared at him angrily. My left cheek stung. I rubbed it gently. I hadn't noticed that the knights had stopped searching and all eyes were on me and my father. "What are you all starring at?" I yelled at them. "I do not have it now go search somewhere else." I demanded them. They all looked at my father for approval. I rolled my eyes again. He nodded his head letting them know that they could leave.

"If I find out you have that necklace Jacintha." He started to say.

"What? You'll kill me father?" I asked in disbelief.

"No Jacintha, you will have a far worse punishment than death." He threatened me.

Riickard came busting through the room with Jaxon. He had Jaxon's arms behind his back. "We found the necklace my lord." he said. My father's face dropped.

Chapter Fifteen

Aletta cried for days. At night, I could hear her cries from my room. She wouldn't speak to our father. She begged him not to put Jaxon in a cell, but he refused.

The whispers around the kingdom were that Jaxon was only using Aletta to get whatever he could get his hands on to sell for money. Aletta didn't believe that at all. She defended him every single day and went down into the dungeon to see him even after father forbidden her to do so. She hardly spoke a word to me as well. I didn't mind it at all. I took pleasure in knowing she wasn't happy. She now feels the misery that I have been feeling since she pushed me down the waterfall.

I still had hope that Jaxon would one day be mine. I had this overall plan leading to his freedom and our successful happy ending. I wanted to wait until Aletta started to lose all hope. I knew she would eventually give up on him. She didn't genuinely love him like I did.

A few weeks have passed, and Aletta was seeing Jaxon less. I knew it was time to make my move. I entered her room where she had on the wedding dress she was supposed to wear.

"Are you okay Aletta?" I asked pretending to care.

"I'm fine Jacintha." she said looking down at her dress with a depressed look on her face.

"Have you spoken to him lately?" I asked.

"No." She put her head down with shame.

"I'm here if you want to talk." I didn't mean it. I didn't want to hear her rant about the man I loved. I still felt vengeance toward her for taking him from me. I knew I had to play nice to get what I wanted in the end.

"I don't want to." she said softly. I didn't want to keep bothering her when I was getting nothing but short answers from her. As I was leaving her room, she started crying. I ran up to her and comforted her. "Why did he lie to me?" she asked, sobbing in her hands.

"I do not know Aletta." I spoke. I didn't know the words to comfort her, nor did I care to.

"He tricked me, and I fell for it. How could I have been so stupid?"

"You are not stupid sister. Jaxon had us all fooled." I told her. "As much as it hurts, you have to let him go."

"I know I do. It's just so hard when all my feelings were real." she said. I never loved another as I did him.

"Our family has gotten through greater loss. We will overcome this as well and you will overcome this heartache." I assured her. Deep down I hoped she felt the pain of losing him every single day of her life.

"Thank you, Jacintha, for being here for me. I don't think we have ever talked like this before. It means a lot to me that we are now." she said as she dried her eyes.

"Now will you please take off that dress. It is making me depressed." I told her and she laughed.

"Of course, I don't know what I was thinking."

"It's okay sister. I must do something quick. I will find you later and we could talk some more." I told her without having any intention of talking to her later.

"Okay. I can't wait." she said with a big smile. As soon as I turned away from her, I rolled my eyes and smiled. If only she knew what I was up to.

I ran down what felt like a hundred steps to where Jaxon was locked up. He looked horrible. He looked as if he hadn't eaten in days and his clothes were filthy. He was shocked to see me.

"Jacintha, what are you doing here?"

"I had to see you Jaxon. I can't believe my father would do this to you."

"You have to believe me Jacintha, I did not take that necklace."

"I do believe you Jaxon. I know you would never do something like that but, my father and Aletta are convinced that you did."

"Aletta thinks I, did it?" he put his head down.

"She has given up on you Jaxon. I knew she wouldn't fight to get you out of here." I convinced him.

"I have to get out of here Jacintha." he told me.

"I have a plan." I pulled the key to the cell out of my pocket.

"Where did you get this?" he asked surprised.

"I took it from Riickard without him knowing."

"Give it to me so I can escape." he anxiously said as he reached for the key in my hand.

I pulled the key back from him so he couldn't reach it. "If you escape now, you will surely die. There are too many guards on the ground. You will be seen." I told him.

"What do you suppose I do?" he asked impatiently.

"Wait until sunset. All the guards will be in one place, and it will be easier to escape. Meet me by the waterfall. There is a way out along the river."

I wasn't positive there was actually a way out through the river. I had never actually passed the waterfall area. If there was, I was going to discover it with Jaxon on our great escape out of here.

"Thank you, Jacintha, for saving me."

"I haven't saved you yet Jaxon." I winked at him.

He had hope once again in his eyes. And that made him have the sexiest eyes ever.

"You saved me once Jaxon, it is the least I can do for you." I told him. I handed him the key. "Just be patient my love. We will be together soon. I kissed him through the bars. My first real kiss. It wasn't how I had always pictured it, but it was magical.

Chapter Sixteen

Back in my room I gathered only what I knew I could carry and waited impatiently for sunset. I couldn't believe how everything was working out so well. Soon I will be off with the love of my life, and we will be long gone before anyone would even notice. I snuck out of the castle without anyone noticing me. As I stood by the waterfall, I grew anxious. Jaxon will be here soon. I imagined the life we would have. We could build our own kingdom and rule it together. Our kids would be happy and never feel like they are in prison. I would love him more than anyone ever has. We would have the happy conclusion we both deserved.

"Waiting for someone?" I heard a familiar voice from behind me say. I quickly turned around and saw Aletta had on a sleeveless byrnie over her shirt. It was funny seeing her like that especially since she always wore dresses. I laughed at the sight of her.

"When I told you to change your dress, I didn't mean for you to put that on." I laughed at her.

"Jaxon isn't coming Jacintha." she said with a serious look on her face.

"What did you do to him?" I grew angry.

"He doesn't want you. He loves me and only me." she said as she revealed her sword from behind her back. I laughed once more.

"So, you plan to kill your unarmed sister? That doesn't seem so fair now does it?"

"I knew you would say that." She threw the sword and it landed on my feet. She quickly grabbed another sword from back.

"Have you forgotten that you aren't any good at sword fights?" I reminded her.

She smirked. "I don't know sister; I think I can manage." she said. She swung at me, and I blocked it. "I know you cut my hair off and blamed it on Hendriick." she said as she took another swing. I blocked that one as well. My foot almost slipped. I knew I was too close to the ledge. She kept swinging and I kept blocking. With each block I pushed forward making sure I wasn't too close to the edge but, she was tougher than I thought. "I know you stole mother's necklace and let Jaxon take the fall for it." She took another swing, and I blocked it. "I know you kissed Jaxon and planned his escape so you can run off with him. It was all a trick, Jacintha. Father and I both know the truth." With every swing she swung I blocked it.

"So, father put you up to this?" I asked. "Did father tell you everything?"

"Father told me all I needed to know." She swung again and missed as usual. I don't know why she would dare challenge me. She knew I was a better swords fighter than she was.

"Did he tell you that I killed our mother for him?" I gave her a devious smile. I knew that would hurt her and I could kill her once and for all. All she was doing was getting in my way. I swung at her but this time I nicked her face. "That's going to leave a scar." I laughed at her.

Aletta froze up and shock went across her face. I saw my opportunity to end her, and I took it. I swung my sword again as hard as I could, but she moved, and I only grazed her arm this time. She cried out in pain as she fell to the ground. I lifted my sword in the air and was about to finish her off when I heard someone yell my name.

"JACINTHA! NO!" Jaxon was running towards us.

"Jaxon." I was hoping he was coming to stop Aletta so we could run off together. I felt a sharp pain in my stomach. My sword fell from my hands as I slowly looked down at my stomach to see my sister's sword going through me. My body grew numb, and it became harder to breathe. My sister stood up from the ground and looked me straight in my eyes. I have never seen such rage in my sister's eyes. She grabbed my shoulders and leaned me into her and whispered, "This is for killing my mother." Then she pushed me off the ledge. I was falling once again. Everyone I knew had betrayed me. How did I not see it would all end like this? No knight in shining armor was going to rescue me. No prince charming could kiss me back to life. No, this was the end.

Acknowledgements

This story was different from any other I had written in the past. It has definitely taken me out of my comfort zone and challenged me as a writer. I enjoyed writing it and I hope you all enjoy reading it.

To my daughter Reyna, thank you for encouraging me to write this story. I had no plans on publishing it, but it was you who convinced me to do so.

To my Frost for all the inspiration. You have brought so many idea's to me. Some good and some bad but always great ideas. I love you always for that.

To my family for all the love you have given me during my journey.

To my kids for all the patience you have given me.

To all my friends for all the support you have given me.

Thank you to everyone who has read my books or has helped promote them in any way shape or form. You all are the greatest and I will forever be grateful for you all. Without all of you I wouldn't have made it this far.

Don't miss out!

Visit the website below and you can sign up to receive emails whenever F. A. Witte publishes a new book. There's no charge and no obligation.

https://books2read.com/r/B-A-SOUM-CQIQC

BOOKS 2 READ

Connecting independent readers to independent writers.

Also by F. A. Witte

Mine
Revenge
The Neighbor
The Fall of Jacintha

Watch for more at https://fawitte08.wixsite.com/fawitte.

About the Author

F. A. Witte was born in Fairview, Oklahoma. She has an associate degree in Medical Assisting. Writing has always been her passion. Starting with poetry, then to short stories, and finally expanding to novels. She has always been a big fan of Poe, King, and Patterson. She likes to get comfortable with a book from any genre when she's not writing, working, or spending time with her family.

Read more at https://fawitte08.wixsite.com/fawitte.